How to
Find Gold

For Kevan

First published 2016 by Walker Books Ltd, 87 Vauxhall Walk, London SE11 5HJ

This edition published 2017

2 4 6 8 10 9 7 5 3 1

© 2016 Viviane Schwarz

The right of Viviane Schwarz to be identified as the author and illustrator of this work has been asserted by her in accordance with the Copyright, Designs and Patents Act 1988

This book has been typeset in ITC Stone Informal

Printed in China

British Library Cataloguing in Publication Data: a catalogue record for this book is available from the British Library

ISBN 978-1-4063-7164-2

www.walker.co.uk

How to Find Gold

VIVIANE SCHWARZ

WALKER BOOKS
AND SUBSIDIARIES
LONDON · BOSTON · SYDNEY · AUCKLAND

"LET'S FIND GOLD," said Anna.

"That would be dangerous and difficult," said Crocodile.

"Good!" said Anna. "Let's go!"

"Wait. Finding gold takes planning," said Crocodile.

"It does?" said Anna.

"No one else can know what we are doing, or they will find it first," said Crocodile. "Look at my face. Can you tell what I am thinking?"

"No."

"That's because I am making a secret face," said Crocodile. "Try it."

"Can you tell what I am thinking?" Anna asked.

"You are thinking about gold."

"And now?"

"Gold."

"Now?"

"Probably still gold," said Crocodile.

"Oh, but you know me very well," said Anna. "It'll do. Let's go!"

"Hang on. Gold is very heavy. We might not be strong enough to carry it," said Crocodile.

"Is it heavier than a crocodile?"

"Probably not," said Crocodile.

"I am strong enough. Where is the gold?"

"Put me down now," said Crocodile. "I will tell you."

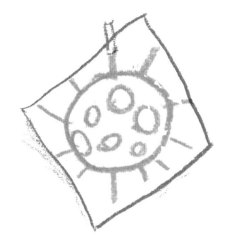

"Gold is always hidden. We need a map with a cross where the gold is," said Crocodile.

"That's easy," said Anna. "Draw a map of the whole world, to be sure."

"It doesn't have a cross," said Crocodile when the map was finished.

Anna drew one on.

"The gold is in France!" said Anna. "How do we get to France?"

"Hm," said Crocodile. "I don't know that bit."

"Not all gold is buried. There is also sunken gold," said Crocodile.

"Let's find that!" said Anna.

"It's even more dangerous and difficult," said Crocodile.

"Good," said Anna.

"Let me explain," said Crocodile. "It is like this."

Crocodile made another drawing.

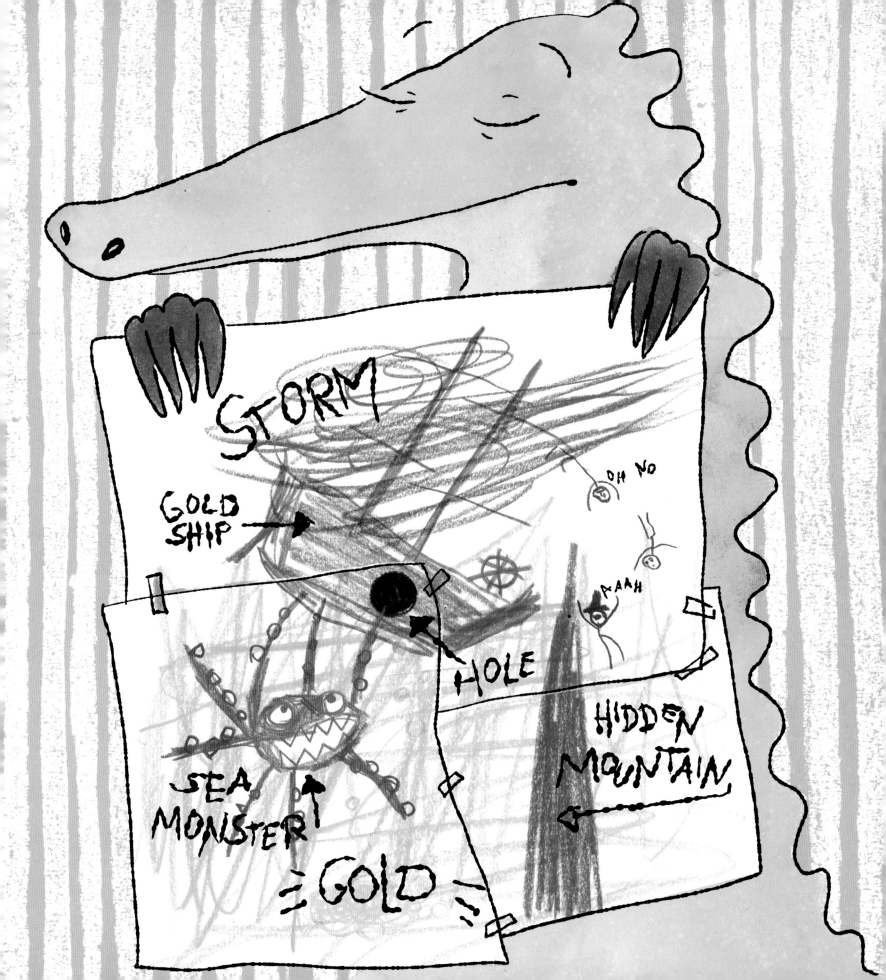

"Wow," said Anna. "Is
it really like that?"

"Yes," said Crocodile.

Anna got the boat.

"Let's find the things
on your drawing,"
she said, "and then
dive for gold."

They went out to sea.

"Where are the ship-sinking mountains?" Anna asked. "Where are the monsters?"

"Underwater," said Crocodile.

Anna looked at the drawing again. "How about holes?"

"They are sunk with the ship," said Crocodile.

"Ah," said Anna. "Finding gold *is* difficult."

"Very," said Crocodile.

"Not dangerous though," said Anna.

"Ha!" said Crocodile. "How about over there, where the sea is boiling and the clouds are like a tower and the fish are in the air?"

"A great storm!" said Anna. "There will be gold!"

"Hold on tight," said Crocodile.

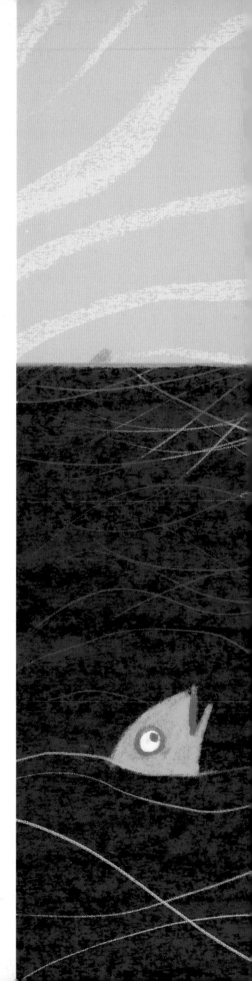

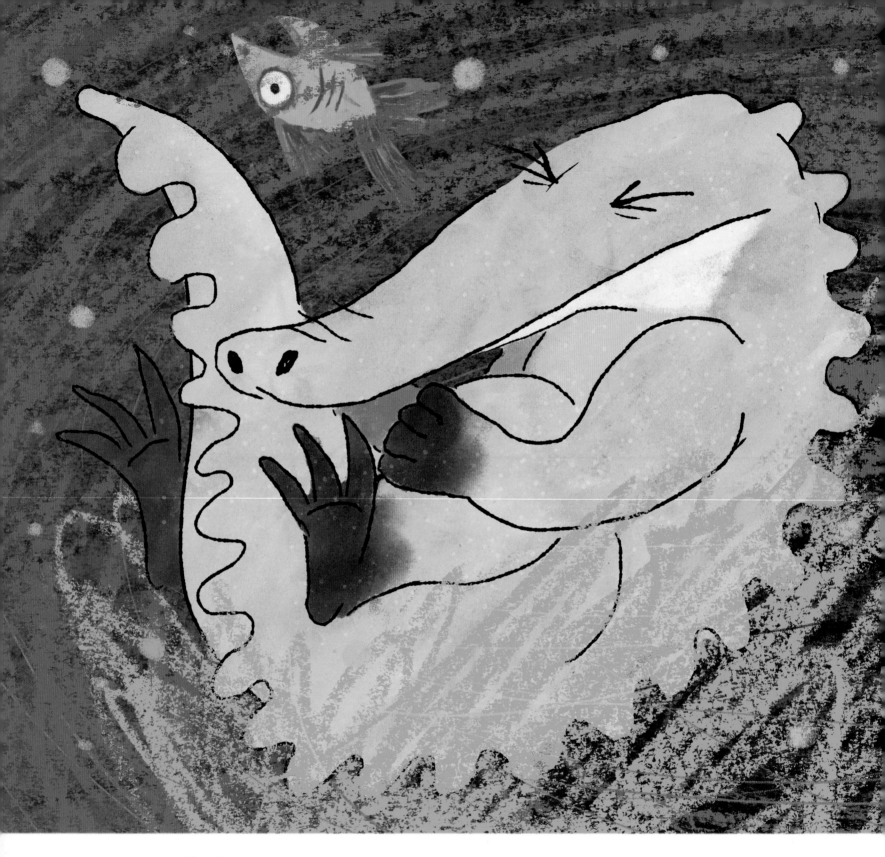

Anna sailed into the great storm and they dived right in the middle.

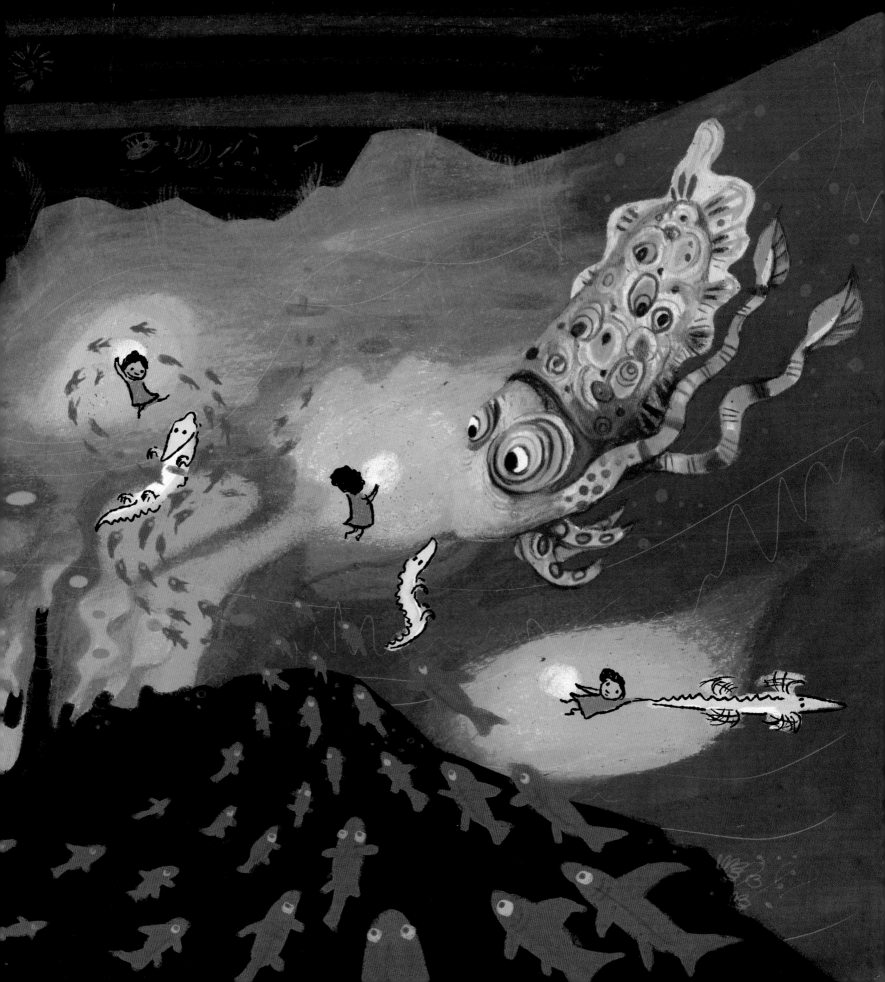

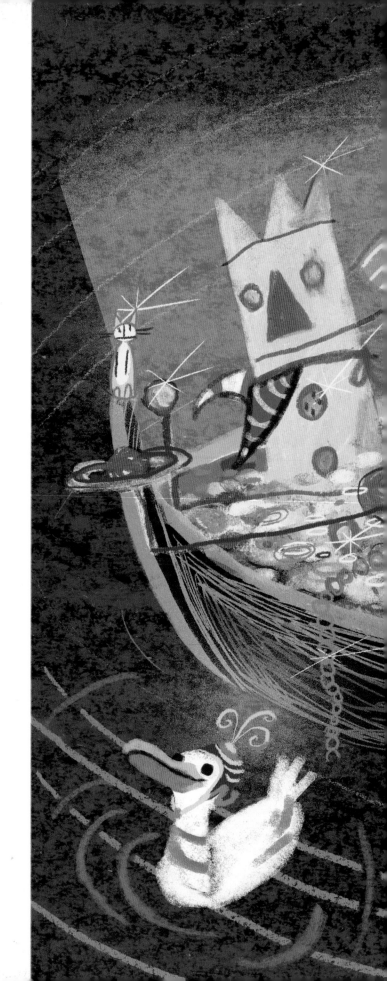

"We have found gold!" said Anna when they could breathe again.

"I don't believe it!" said Crocodile.

"Gold!" said Anna.

"What will we do with it?" asked Crocodile.

"If we spend it," said Anna, "people will know that we have gold."

"That's true. Also, spending it would get rid of the gold," said Crocodile.

"Let's not spend the gold," said Anna.

"Let's hide it," said Crocodile.

"Let's bury it," said Anna, "and draw a map."

"Remember to make a cross on it," said Crocodile.

"This is a very good map," said Crocodile.

"Let's hide it with the gold," said Anna.

"That is safest," Crocodile agreed.

They went home.

"You can stop making the secret face now," said Anna. "No one will ever find our gold."

"This is my happy face, actually," said Crocodile. "It just looks similar."

Anna made her happy face, too.

"We found gold," she said. "It was dangerous and difficult."

"But now it is ours for ever," said Crocodile.

And it was.